Herman Melville's

Moby Dick

Retold For Kids

(Beginner Reader Classics)

Max James

KidLit-O Press

www.KidLito.com

Cover Image © moleskostudio - Fotolia.com

D0696817

Table of Contents

About

KidLit-o was started for one simple reason: our kids. They wanted to find a way to introduce classic literature to their children.

Books in this series take all the classics that they love and make them age appropriate for a younger audience—while still keeping the integrity and style of the original.

We hope you and you children enjoy them. We love feedback, so if you have a question or comment, stop by our website!

Chapter 1: The Captain and his Crew

Long ago, in a town called Nantucket in the state of Massachusetts, there lived an old, eccentric sea captain named Ahab. He was a captain of whale hunting ships. He hunted a special kind of whale, an extremely large, absolutely gigantic species of whale, generally of a dark color, for its oil. A year before the beginning of this story, Captain Ahab had been on a voyage during which he had lost his leg to a whale, a totally unique whale. Even though this whale was of the generally dark species Ahab hunted, he was pure white! As a result, he became known simply as "the White Whale". Another name he came to be known by was "Moby-Dick". Nobody knows who invented the latter name! It just emerged, and was passed from storyteller to storyteller as the legend grew.

After the poor man lost his leg, he became terribly sad and depressed. Later on, he became what many people considered crazy! A leg of whale ivory was made for him, and he became known for the sound of his walk. The "click, click, click". His new leg enabled him to continue going to sea, and he soon engaged himself as captain on a whaling ship named "The Pequod". The Pequod was a regular whaling ship, like any other. The owners of the ship, Captains Peleg and Bildad, chose Ahab because of his forty years of whaling experience. They did not know that he had a specific purpose in mind, a purpose outside of what they intended for their ship. They would not have approved, and so he held his monumental secret closely to his chest.

The Pequod was staffed with many men, from all over the world. The most prominent personages, aside the captain, were the three mates and the three harpooners. The first (or chief, and therefore highest ranking) mate was named Starbuck. Like Ahab, he was from Nantucket, while unlike Ahab, he was remarkably sensible and level-headed. As such, he considered an utterly fearless man far more dangerous a comrade than a coward, and was moderate and conscientious in all things. His father and brother had been killed in the whale fishery, and he did not wish to inflict the same grief upon his wife and small child waiting at home. He was a thin yet strong and quite handsome man of about thirty years of age.

The second mate was Stubb, a good-humored but careless man from Cape Cod. He faced dangers with an indifferent air, as if the thought of the possibility of death had never occurred to him. He constantly smoked tobacco from a small, black pipe. He smoked it so consistently that he was never seen without it! Many of the men thought he might put his pipe in his mouth before putting his trousers on in the morning!

A man named Flask was the third mate. This short, stout, and ruddy young man was from Martha's Vineyard. Like Stubb, he tended to be careless and unaware of the danger around him. In fact, he surpassed Stubb in his fearlessness, which seemed to stem from simple ignorance. He lacked any sense of reverence for the size, power, and beauty of his prey. These characteristics combined made him prone to showing off and acting as if he were capable of killing three whales at once, single-handedly!

As in all whaling ships, the three mates each commanded one of the Pequod's boats, as headsmen. For, when hunting whales, the men had to get closer to the whales than staying on the ship could afford. In each boat, the mates would carry lances as weapons. The harpooners, however, were the men who first attacked the whale, flinging metal harpoons with rope attached. The three harpooners were Queequeg, Tashtego, and Daggoo. They were brave, generous, and honest men.

Queequeg, a native of the Polynesian islands, was a remarkably large, formidable looking man, covered in traditional tattoos. He was the harpooner of Starbuck's boat crew. Although some found his appearance frightening, he was a loyal, intelligent, and reasonable man, as was Tashtego, Stubb's harpooner. Tashtego was a Native American, with long black hair, black eyes, and a devilish slender, flexible build. His agility and skill were remarkable. While Tashtego most benefited from his slender, lean quickness, Daggoo, Flask's harpooner, was a giant of a man. He was six foot five and incredible in his bulk. He was African and wore two large golden hoops in his ears. It was extremely odd that he should be under little Flask's command, and the discrepancy in the two men's sizes was a source of mirth amongst the crew!

There were so many men aboard the Pequod that to endeavor a description of all would take more pages than any book could contain! Only one more can we select for mention. A New Englander like the ship's captain and mates, a mysterious man called Ishmael formed part of the crew. His only previous sailing experience had been on merchant ships, and this was, therefore, his first whaling voyage. He was great friends with Queequeg. Many of the crew suspected he underestimated the perils of a whaling voyage, and would be in for many surprises. They were right.

Chapter 2: Ahab's Emergence

For the first few days of the Pequod's voyage, Ahab was nowhere to be seen by the harpooners and men. The three mates indeed saw him, when they went into his cabin to receive orders. They saw his lean but spiritually strong appearance, his grey hair, and his floppy black hat, as well as the unusual, long bright white scar that started on the side of his face and extended down his neck and shirt. They became acquainted with his strange ways.

However, Ahab's absence caused immense speculation among the crew. Was he ill? Was he dead? Was he not even on the ship at all? They had heard that the captain was eccentric, but this kind of behavior from a captain was unheard of. Luckily, one night Ahab decided to emerge from his cabin. Only Stubb and a few of the men on night watch duty witnessed this marvel. Everyone else had to wait until the next day for the privilege.

The night he first emerged, the old man made his way up from his cabin with difficulty, gripping at the iron bannister. He began to walk on a sort of patrol on deck. His ivory leg, of course, made its sound, its click, click, click, and could be heard down below by the previously sleeping Stubb! Very annoyed at being woken, Stubb angrily reached the deck and confronted Ahab. He asked the captain if there were any means of muffling the sound. Ahab became angry.

"Am I a cannon-ball, Stubb, that you would wad me in that fashion? But go your way. I had forgotten. Below to the nightly grave of sleep. Down, dog, and kennel!"

Stubb was absolutely stunned, and extremely offended, by this speech. He took a moment to collect himself, and then proceeded to answer.

"I am not used to being spoken to in that way, sir. I must say that I do not like it, sir."

Ahab flew into a fury! "Avast! Begone!" he gritted between his set teeth. He then moved away, as if to avoid some violent temptation.

Stubb felt emboldened. "I will not be tamely called a dog, sir," he asserted.

Ahab seemed to only just barely control himself. His eyes were on fire. He took a deep breath and then replied, "Then be called a donkey and a mule, and begone, or I'll rid the world of you!" Ahab then stepped towards the mate in such a frightening manner that Stubb involuntarily retreated.

Ahab, after a few minutes of calming himself, stood for a while leaning over the side of the ship, looking at the sea. He then lit his pipe, sat on a stool, and smoked. He began to speak, even though he was alone. "This smoking no longer soothes. Oh, my pipe! Hard and unjust must it go with me if I no longer feel thy charm! I have been smoking with nervous whiffs, like a dying whale whose final jets are the strongest and fullest of trouble. What business do I have with this pipe? This thing that is meant for serenity, to send up mild vapors among mild white hairs, not iron-grey locks like mine. I'll smoke no more." He then tossed the pipe into the sea.

Chapter 3: Ahab's Announcement

One morning, Ahab ordered Starbuck to assemble the entire crew on deck. Starbuck did so. Everyone was quite nervous. Ahab's unpredictable nature was by this point well known. It seemed he wanted to make an announcement! What could it be? The captain began to speak, loudly, clearly, and intensely.

"All ye mast-headers have heard me speak of a white whale." He held up a gold coin. "Do you see this Spanish ounce of gold?" He held the coin to the sun. "Do you see it?" The crew nervously assented. "The man who raises me a white whale with a wrinkled brow, a crooked jaw, and three holes punctured in his body, shall have this gold ounce!"

"Huzza! Huzza!" cried the seamen.

"It's a white whale, remember," resumed Ahab. "Look sharp for white water. If you see a bubble, call out!"

When Ahab mentioned the white whale, with its wrinkled brow and crooked jaw, the three harpooners, Tashtego, Queequeg, and Daggoo, gave looks of recognition and surprise. Tashtego soon spoke out.

"Captain Ahab, that white whale you spoke of must be Moby-Dick!"

Ahab responded with a look and cry of exaltation. "Moby Dick? Do you know the White Whale, Tash?"

Daggoo spoke up, as well. "Does he have a curious spout? Very quick?"

Queequeg joined in. "Does he have one, two, three, oh, a good many irons in him, Captain?"

"Yes! Yes! That is he! Aye, those irons are mine! This is the White Whale, who took my leg. This is what we are here for, men! It was Moby-Dick who brought me to this dead stump I stand on now! I will have vengeance!" cried the jubilant captain. "God bless you, men!"

Starbuck felt terribly worried and justifiably fearful. Captain Ahab could see this on his face. "Why the sad face, Mr. Starbuck?" asked Ahab.

Starbuck paused for a moment, and then responded. "Captain Ahab, I came here to hunt whales, not for my commander's vengeance. How many barrels of oil will your vengeance yield?"

Ahab looked pale with anger. Starbuck continued.

"Vengeance on a dumb animal, an animal that acts simply on instinct! This is madness!" Starbuck said, as calmly as he could.

Ahab walked away.

Chapter 4: Phantoms

Although Ahab's only goal on this voyage was to carry out vengeance on Moby-Dick, he knew that if he forbade his men from hunting other whales and thus finding oil and an income, they might rebel. Therefore, he allowed them to hunt other whales, but took very little interest in the pursuit. Every other whaling ship the Pequod encountered was assailed with Ahab's question: "hast thou seen the White Whale?" While some had seen him, many had not. He had no interest in any other information.

One day, a whale was spotted, and the hunt was initiated. Everyone on the ship except for Ahab thought there would only be three boats. Suddenly, however, Ahab emerged with five men that had never been seen before by anyone on the ship! How they suddenly appeared there, in the middle of the ocean, no one knew. The logical conclusion was that Ahab had smuggled them on before the beginning of the voyage, but everyone was so surprised they were not thinking logically. The five men seemed like phantoms. They were Asian and were dressed in black. One of them had an especially supernatural, otherworldly air to his appearance and presence. His name was Fedallah, and he was from Persia. He was an adherent of an East Indian religion that the crew were ignorant of, and, therefore, they later came to simply call him the Parsee, without knowing what it meant. He was tall and appeared rather old. He wore a crumpled, black Chinese jacket. Although all his clothes were black, he wore a glistening white turban. His long hair was braided and coiled underneath. The other mysterious men appeared to be from various countries of East Asia. Ahab spoke.

"All ready, Fedallah?"

"Ready," replied Fedallah. His quiet, unearthly voice sounded almost like a hiss.

Chapter 5: Stubb Kills a Whale

It was a sultry and sleepy day when Stubb killed his first whale of the voyage. Until the said whale appeared, the whole crew was in a dreamy, enchanted mood. Suddenly, Ishmael spotted an especially gigantic whale near the ship. The whale seemed to be in the same dreamy mood as the men. He appeared supremely relaxed, and the periodic spouting of his vapory jet made him resemble a well-fed gentleman meditatively smoking his pipe on a warm afternoon. When Ishmael notified the rest of the crew of this whale's presence, the whole ship started into wakefulness and action.

At first Ahab and his mates suspected that the whale had heard the commotion and would be alarmed and aware of its pursuit but after they lowered the boats they realized that while the whale was swimming away, he was doing so in a tranquil manner. It was clear that he was not yet aware of the pursuit.

Consequently, Ahab ordered that the men be as quiet as possible, and to paddle with their hands instead of their oars and talk in whispers. All of a sudden, however, the whale flitted his tail forty feet in the air and then sank down deep into the water.

Stubb realized a wait would be involved, and lit his pipe in order to relax in the interval. Shortly afterward, the whale rose again and was now in advance of Stubb's boat. It was much nearer to that boat than any other. In a rather pompous voice, Stubb addressed his boat crew: "I believe I can count upon the honor of this capture." Soon, he turned to his harpooner, Tashtego, and shouted "Stand up, Tashtego! Throw the harpoon!" In compliance with this order, Tashtego stood up and joyfully hurled the harpoon. The whale, of course, was in great agitation and distress, and the water foamed with bubbles as if it were boiling. The whale attempted to escape, but soon lost the energy needed to do so. Stubb soon cried "Haul in! Haul in!" All the oarsmen began pulling the boat closer to the whale. The water was red with the poor, tormented animal's blood. The sun was shining upon the water, and caused the color of the blood to reflect back on the men's faces, which was terribly unsettling. It indicated that

Stubb and his men had a terrific deal of blood on their hands and consciences. If this thought occurred to anyone, it was quickly dismissed, and the persecution continued. Jet after jet of white smoke was agonizingly shot from the spiracle of the whale, while Stubb's pipe released puff after puff. Stubb soon cried "Pull up! Pull up!", and all his men pulled the boat closer to the whale. Stubb then reached far over the side and slowly stabbed the whale with his long sharp lance. He kept it in the whale, churning it around as if he were looking for some gold watch that the whale had swallowed. It was soon realized that the animal's heart had burst. He was dead. This fact was first announced by Tashtego. He said, "He's dead, Mr. Stubb." Stubb replied, "Yes, both pipes smoked out!" Stubb then withdrew his pipe and scattered its ashes over the water. He then stared at the corpse he had made.

That evening, Stubb let it be known that he wished to eat a whale steak! He put poor Daggoo into peril by making him clamber down to the whale still hanging alongside the ship and cut the steak, and then forced the ship's extremely elderly cook, Fleece, to cook it. When poor old Fleece presented the dish to Stubb, the mate expressed dissatisfaction. "Cook, don't you think this steak is rather overdone? You've also made it too tender!" Fleece was extremely surprised at this statement, as the meat was quite red and rare. Stubb continued, "A whale-steak must be tough! Look at the sharks now over the side. They prefer it tough and rare!" Stubb paused and listened for a moment. "What a fuss those sharks are kicking up! Cook, go and speak to them. Tell them they must keep quiet! Take my lantern. Go and preach to them!"

Fleece took the lantern and slowly made his way to the side of the ship where the dead whale and sharks were located. He leaned over the side, and proceeded to speak to them. Stubb quietly followed him, as he intended to amuse himself at the cook's expense!

Fleece addressed the sharks. "Critters, I've been ordered to say you must stop that noise there! You hear? Stop that smackin' of the lips!" Suddenly, Fleece heard Stubb laugh behind him. He turned, and saw Stubb making his way back to his meal with great mirth.

Chapter 6: Gabriel

It was a breezy day, so much so that the Pequod began to rock. Soon, another American whale ship came into view and approached the Pequod. It was the Jeroboam of Nantucket, a ship that was suffering a terrible epidemic. The ship's captain, Captain Mayhew, wanted to avoid infecting the Pequod's crew. Although Mayhew and his individual boat crew were not infected, he refused to allow himself or anyone else from his boat board the Pequod. However, he and Ahab were able to carry on a conversation from a rifle-shot's distance. This was made a bit difficult by two circumstances. Firstly, the contrary wind sometimes would push ahead either the ship or boat out of shouting distance, and secondly, there was a truly strange man onboard the Jeroboam boat who continually interrupted the conversation. This man was known as "Gabriel," and he had managed to gain a great deal of power on the ship through making most of the crew believe he had supernatural powers bestowed by God!   He was a youngish, small man with yellow hair and freckles. His eyes betrayed a fanatic delirium. He had originally joined a whaling expedition on a strange, religiously inspired whim. He had managed to seem sane until the ship was far from land, at which point he announced himself as the archangel Gabriel and commanded his captain to jump overboard! He declared himself ruler of all Oceanica! The captain had quietly planned to rid himself of this strange prophet by leaving him at a port, but the crew soon told him that if Gabriel were sent away, they would all desert the expedition! This is the extent to which Gabriel had instilled awe and fear in the majority of the ship's men. When the epidemic broke out, Gabriel had declared that this "plague" was under his control and that he, and only he, could end it. Many of the crew paid homage to him as a god and begged for his benevolence and mercy.

"I do not fear your epidemic, man," said Captain Ahab to Captain Mayhew. "Come on board."

Gabriel jumped to his feet. "Think, think of the horrible plague!"

A wave shot the boat far ahead. When it drifted back, Ahab asked his wonted question: "Have you seen the White Whale?" Before Mayhew had time to answer, Gabriel spoke again. "Think, think of the whale-boat, destroyed and sunk! Think of the horrible tail!"

Captain Mayhew began to tell a frightening story concerning Moby-Dick, but was frequently interrupted by Gabriel and the waves that sometimes pushed the boat ahead. Mayhew explained that shortly after beginning their voyage, they met another whale ship that warned them of Moby-Dick's ferocity and the damage he had done. Taking advantage of this information, Gabriel had immediately declared that terrible things should befall anyone who attempted to kill this mighty whale.

Later in the voyage, Moby-Dick was spotted from the Jeroboam's mastheads, and Macey, the chief mate, became determined to hunt him. He persuaded five men to join him for this adventure. The end result of all of this was that Moby-Dick knocked the boat so violently from underneath where Macey sat, that the mate was thrown high into the air. He then fell into the sea and could not be recovered. Gabriel was secretly thrilled at this result. It gave his claim of being a formidable, powerful prophet greater credibility in the eyes of many of the crew.

After Mayhew had finished telling this Moby-Dick story to Ahab, he asked the captain whether he himself intended to hunt the whale. Ahab, of course, immediately answered "Aye." At this point, Gabriel again leapt up, glared at Ahab, and shouted "Think, think of the blasphemer! Dead, and down there! Beware his end!" Ahab ignored this outburst, and said to Mayhew, "Captain, I have just remembered there is a letter for one of your officers in our letter bag." He then sent Starbuck to find the letter.

When Starbuck returned with the letter, Ahab declared it was for Macey, the dead mate!

"Poor fellow! It is from his wife," lamented Mayhew. "But let me have it."

"No, you must keep it," cried Gabriel at Ahab. "You will soon go his way."

"Curses throttle you!" yelled Ahab. Ahab put the letter in the slit of a pole, and reached it towards where Captain Mayhew sat in the boat. However, a wave moved the boat unexpectedly, and the letter landed on Gabriel's hand. He impaled the letter on a boat-knife and threw it back onto the Pequod.

Chapter 7: Tashtego's Accident

One day, brave Tashtego had a horrifying accident! He was in the process of harvesting the contents of a whale's head, an object at least twenty feet in length! To do so, he was balanced on the top of the head, which was secured beside the ship and touching the surface of the water. He retrieved bucket after bucket of the contents and sent them up to the waiting crew. During all this time, he secured his safety by hanging with one arm on the great cable suspending the head. Suddenly, after the eightieth or ninetieth bucket, poor Tashtego somehow lost hold of the cable and fell head first into the whale's enormous head! With a horrible oily gurgling, he went totally out of sight! Everyone was stunned with horror for a moment. Then, Daggoo cried, "Man overboard! Give me the bucket!"

The men transported Daggoo to the very top of the head while Tashtego must have been sinking to the bottom. Everyone who looked over the side could see the head throbbing and heaving just below the surface of the sea as if at that moment seized with an idea. It was poor Tashtego's struggling that was causing these movements. This showed how far he had sunk.

Suddenly, one of the two hooks suspending the head failed. There was now only one hook holding up the enormous object. Daggoo began to push the bucket down into the head, thinking that Tashtego could take hold of it and then be pulled out. Stubb is staring in amazement and alarm.

"Stop this! What are you doing, man? How will doing that help him? You're jamming an iron-bound bucket on top of him!" Stubb exclaimed.

Almost at that moment, the monumental head fell into the sea! Through a thick mist of spray, Daggoo could be faintly seen clinging to the cable while the unfortunate Tashtego was buried alive and sinking to the bottom of the sea! Soon, through the mist could be seen another figure. It was Queequeg, holding a sword. He dove into the sea. Some of the men lowered a boat and hovered in the area. Moments passed, and there was no sign of either Queequeg or Tashtego! Then, suddenly, an arm was thrust forth from the water.

"It is both men!" cried Daggoo, joyfully.

Soon, heroic Queequeg was seen emerging, with one hand clutching Tashtego's long hair.

Chapter 8: The Unscrupulous Captain

One day, the Pequod met a German whaling ship called the Jungfrau. Its captain, Derick De Deer, seemed extremely anxious to make the acquaintance of the Pequod's captain and crew. While still some distance from the Pequod, the Jungfrau dropped a boat. The captain was standing in it, holding a mysterious object. As his boat moved closer and closer to the Pequod, the three mates, Starbuck, Stubb, and Flask, discussed what the object might be.

"What does he have in his hand there?" asked Starbuck. He peered more closely. "Impossible! A lamp feeder? A whale ship, that hunts the source of the best oil, must beg for oil from another ship?"

"No," answered Stubb. "No, I believe it's a coffee pot. He's coming to make our coffee," he joked.

"No. It's a lamp-feeder and oil can. He's come for our oil!" exclaimed Flask.

The German captain finally reached the Pequod and mounted the deck. Without offering any sort of greeting or pleasantry, or asking about the object in De Deer's hand, Ahab abruptly asked him if he had seen the White Whale. Captain De Deer explained, in broken English, that he had never heard of such a whale. De Deer immediately began to talk about his lamp feeder and oil can. Ahab had no interest in this conversation and so immediately and rudely departed, leaving his three mates to deal with the visitor.

Oil was given to the German captain, and he departed. By the time his boat reached the side of the Jungfrau, several whales almost simultaneously appeared and were seen from the mast-heads of both ships. As the Jungfrau had not caught even one whale on the whole of its journey, De Deer enthusiastically turned his boat in chase, without even putting his lamp feeder and oil can aboard his ship. Three other boats were soon lowered from the German ship and followed in pursuit. The three Pequod's mates' boats were lowered, as well. Soon, it was clear that all boats, both American and German, were pursuing a single whale. This whale was much slower than the rest of the pod, which had sped off at such a rate that their capture seemed out of the question for that day.

At this point, Captain De Deer's boat was in the lead but was closely approached by its American rivals. De Deer seemed remarkably confident of his victory, and, as a derisive gesture, shook his lamp feeder at the American boats!

"The ungracious and ungrateful dog!" exclaimed Starbuck.

A little later, the German captain became even more insulting when he proceeded to throw his lamp-feeder and oil can at the advancing American boats!

"The unmannerly dog!" shouted Stubb.

The German captain's rude and ungrateful behavior made the Americans so angry that their speed and position soon almost matched De Deer's. De Deer would still have won the race, but for the fact that a crab became caught in the blade of one of his oarsmen! While the German men struggled with this problem, their captain became enraged, and their boat almost capsized! Meanwhile, the American boats easily caught up.

In a panic, De Deer ordered his harpooner to stand up. But this harpooner's speed could have hoped to match that of Queequeg, Tashtego, and Daggoo, who stood up and hurled their harpoons before the German harpooner had even gained his balance. Their harpoons flew right over the heads of De Deer and his boat crew. All three harpoons successfully hit the whale.

Chapter 9: In the Eye of the Storm

The Pequod was now in the waters of southeast Asia, heading towards Japan. Captain Ahab every day became more hopeful of seeing his fearsome White Whale. Whales were known to congregate in large groups in this part of the world, at this time of the year.

Soon, an extensive herd was spotted, at a long distance. Numerous whale jets could be seen on the horizon, sparkling in the early afternoon air. At Ahab's direction, the Pequod immediately increased speed. Soon, Ahab noticed white vapors in the far distance behind the ship. He turned quickly and looked in that direction with his glass. What he saw made him start in alarm. He saw a ship of Malaysian pirates!

"More speed! Pirates in pursuit!" he shouted.

The crew immediately scrambled to carry out the order. They managed to sail so quickly that they passed through to much broader waters beyond, and the pirates either lost track of them or decided catching them wasn't worth the effort. Whatever the reason, the Pequod was now safe. The men rejoiced at this, and even more so at the fact that they were now much closer to the whales. However, when they were still a mile away from the whales, the herd, by some incredible instinct, became aware of the ship in pursuit of them and formed into organized, military-like ranks!

It is to be presumed that Ahab did not spot his White Whale, as he did not lower his boat. The three mates' boats were lowered and went off towards the whales. They chased the animals for several hours! When the mates were almost ready to give up, the whales were suddenly driven to indecisiveness and disorganization by panic. The military form they had previously held now slipped into chaos. Whales swam in different directions.

Within a few minutes, Starbuck's boat was in a position to try for a whale, and Queequeg was ordered to fling his harpoon. The whale it hit was terribly frightened and in pain and swam powerfully for the heart of the herd! As a consequence, Starbuck and his men were caught in the very middle of the chaotic scene, while the other boats remained on the edges. However, it is said that an enchanted calm exists at the heart of every commotion, and Starbuck's crew found this to be true. At first, the men were seriously alarmed, but when they realized that most of the whales near them were female and juvenile whales, they felt calmer. They would not kill any of these whales, for fear of the consequences. They might be attacked and swamped by the group at large. So, they sat in their boat as quietly as possible. Soon, female, mother and baby whales came to visit them, as tamely as pet dogs. Queequeg patted their heads, and Starbuck scratched their backs!

Chapter 10: Pip

On whale ships, there were always a certain number of people who acted only as "ship-keepers" and never, or almost never, went into the boats. A young and slender teenage African-American boy who went by the nicknames "Pippin" and "Pip" was one of this group on the Pequod. He was a remarkably intelligent, pleasant, and jolly boy.

On one occasion, one of Stubb's oarsmen sprained his hand, and could not carry out his function. Pip was chosen to temporarily take his place. Pip met this news with some fear and a vast deal of nervousness.

On his first lowering, Pip was terribly anxious, but as he managed to escape close contact with the whale and, therefore, showed little fear, he received Stubb's praise. However, on his second lowering, the whale happened to be right under Pip's seat when it was darted. The whale's violent movement caused Pip to leap out of the boat in fear! In this process, his neck somehow became entangled with the whale line!

Tashtego looked at Pip extremely angrily. He realized that they would have to cut the line and then the whale would go free. He snatched a boat knife and suspended it over the line. He asked Stubb, "Cut?" Pip's face was now turning blue! Stubb turned bright red in anger. "Cut!" he roared. All of this happened remarkably quickly, in less than half a minute. The whale, of course, escaped.

After they had returned to the ship, Stubb had a stern talk with Pip. He warned him that if he ever jumped again, he would be left stranded!

Pip hoped for the best on his third lowering. However, his control over himself in the presence of a monstrous whale seemed sorely lacking! He jumped again! This time he was not entangled with the line, however, and Stubb simply continued following the whale, leaving Pip stranded in the ocean! Now, Stubb did not mean for him to be stranded forever. He assumed that one of the other boats would soon pick him up. As it happened, though, the other boats spotted another whale in a different direction, and did not see Pip floundering in the water!

Poor Pip was in a terrifying situation. He was absolutely alone, in the middle of an immense ocean. No matter which direction he looked, he saw nothing but water and sky! The panic that he felt was overwhelming. Since he had no method of keeping track of the time, he was unsure as to how much time passed. To him, it seemed a literal eternity. He was rescued at last by the ship, entirely by chance! What would poor Pip have done if chance had gone against him? This question, in addition to all the immense questions that passed through his head while stranded, had two effects on the poor child. The first was that he was traumatized psychologically, and some men thought he had a sort of madness. The second was that he had gained a special wisdom, a wisdom that comes from looking at death. He was never the same Pip again.

Chapter 11: The Samuel Enderby, of London

One day, the Pequod met a ship named the Samuel Enderby of London, England. While some of his officers called this ship's captain "Captain Boomer," it was not clear whether this was his actual name or whether it was said in jest. This is because so much was said in jest upon the English ship! The English captain was about Ahab's age but appeared in better health and had an ivory arm! He was darkly tanned, burly, and good looking. His looks and expression gave the impression of a good natured temperament, and that ended up being a correct assumption. He as laid back, jolly, and kind. Even though, like Ahab, he had lost a limb to a whale, he did not have any of Ahab's pointless determination for vengeance.

After Ahab had asked this captain if he had seen the White Whale, and the captain answered yes, he had, and not only that, that Moby-Dick was the whale who took his arm, Captain Ahab was in a state of strange excitement and was determined to speak to this fellow victim. He hastily rushed into a boat to travel over to the Samuel Enderby, failing to consider that the English ship lacked the equipment the Pequod had to help him get on board! Luckily, when he got to the side of the English ship, the ship's crew improvised and found a way to get the captain on board. The stranger captain looked at Ahab's leg and said, "I see, I see," and he and his crew created the already mentioned improvisation.

Once Ahab made it aboard, the only subject he wished to discuss was, as always, the White Whale. He was frustrated to find that Moby-Dick was not the only topic of conversation aboard the Samuel Enderby. In fact, the English captain preferred not to dwell upon the subject. Unlike Ahab, he realized that no amount of brooding or vengeance would get his arm back, and, therefore, it was fruitless. He did not have Ahab's crazed focus on one fixed idea and goal.

"Where did you see the White Whale? How long ago?" asked Ahab.

The English captain sadly pointed his ivory arm towards the East. "There I saw him, to the East. Last season."

"And he took that arm off?" asked Ahab.

"Yes. He was the cause of it, at least," the English captain replied. He looked down at Ahab's ivory leg. "And that leg, too?"

Ahab nodded grimly. There were a few moments of silence.

The English captain continued. "He pulled my arm off. We had secured him with the harpoon. He was so incredibly strong and large (he was the largest whale I had ever seen!) that his flailings were terrible and especially dangerous. The only think I could think to do to protect myself was, oddly, grabbing hold of my harpoon-pole sticking in him! I clung to it. But suddenly the whale took a dart forwards and then dove deep. The barb of the iron caught me just below my shoulder. As he dragged me down, my arm was quickly ripped off entirely."

At this point, the English captain invited the ship's surgeon, Dr. Bunger, to join the conversation.

"It was a terribly bad wound," said Dr. Bunger. "I had to be very severe with the captain with regard to his diet!"

"Oh, very severe!" the captain said, laughing. He altered his voice, so it seemed he might not be saying something entirely serious or true, and was only joking. In order words, he was being facetious! "Drinking hot rum toddies with me every evening, till he couldn't see to put on the bandages, and sending me to bed about three o'clock in the morning! Oh yes, severe and fastidious."

The surgeon decided to join in the joviality. "Ah, my captain spins many clever stories of this sort. , I never touch alcohol." Dr. Bunger then slightly turned, to hide his smile.

All this good-humored talk was boring Ahab, and he was becoming impatient. He suddenly spat out, "What became of the White Whale?"

"Oh, oh yes!" cried the English captain. "Well, we didn't see him again for some time."

"Did you see him again," asked Ahab.

"Twice."

"But could not catch him?" asked Ahab.

"Didn't want to try. Isn't losing one limb enough? What should I do without my one remaining arm? No, no. No more White Whales for me! There would be great glory in killing him, I know, but he's best left alone. Don't you agree, Captain Ahab?" The English captain then glanced at Ahab's ivory leg.

"He is. But I will hunt him. How long since you last saw him? Which direction was he heading in?"

"Bless my soul, this man's blood! It's at the boiling point! Where is my thermometer? His pulse makes the planks we stand on beat!" exclaimed Dr. Bunger.

Ahab ignored him disdainfully, and repeated his question. "Which way heading?"

The English captain stared at Ahab in amazement, and was stunned silent for a moment. He then said, "Good grief! What's the matter?" Ahab didn't answer. "He was heading east, I think." The English captain then leaned over to Fedallah and whispered, "Is your captain crazy?" Fedallah responded by putting a finger before his lip. He then mysteriously slid over the side and easily found his way into Ahab's boat.

Ahab was, with great difficulty, placed back in his boat. His anger and impatience, however, led him to make frustrated, angry movements. He soon broke his ivory leg!

When he returned to the Pequod, he immediately summoned the ship's carpenter and blacksmith. They were ordered to make him a new leg by morning!

Chapter 12: Starbuck's First Confrontation with Ahab

The next morning, Starbuck discovered there were leaks in at least some of the oil casks. A considerable amount of oil had been lost! He immediately went down to Captain Ahab's cabin, to report the circumstance. He advised Ahab to anchor the ship for a week in order to repair the casks.

"What? We are near Japan, but you would like us to stay here for a week to tinker with old casks?" asked Ahab.

Starbuck expressed surprise at this speech. He paused for a moment, and then continued. "Either we do that, sir, or waste in one day more oil than we may make in a year. That which we came twenty thousand miles to get is worth saving, sir."

"Yes, it is, if we get it," said Ahab.

"I was referring to the oil in the hold, sir," replied Starbuck.

"And I was not speaking or thinking of the oil at all," responded Ahab.

"The White Whale," said Starbuck, quietly and grimly.

"Begone! Let it leak!" shouted Ahab.

"What will the ship's owners say, sir?" asked Starbuck.

"Who cares about the owners? Owners, owners? You are always harping on about such things. The owners are not my conscience. In any case, the only real owner of a ship is its captain and commander! Now, be gone. On deck!" exclaimed Ahab.

Starbuck's face reddened. He paused, and began to speak more slowly and cautiously. "Captain Ahab, your age and sadness make this easier for me to forbear."

Ahab flew into a fury. "Do you dare to criticize me?" he yelled. He then grabbed a loaded musket from the rack and pointed it at Starbuck! He shouted "There is one captain that is lord over the Pequod. On deck!"

Starbuck felt terribly angry and insulted, but controlled his emotions. He said quietly, "Let Ahab beware of Ahab. Beware of thyself, old man." He then turned around and promptly left the cabin. Ahab began to mutter to himself.

"He waxes brave, but still obeys. That is a most careful bravery! What did he say? Ahab beware of Ahab. Perhaps there's something to that."

Ahab unconsciously began to use his musket as a walking staff. He paced his cabin. After a time, the thick wrinkles in his forehead relaxed. He put the gun away, and then went to the deck. He found Starbuck.

"You are too good a fellow, Starbuck," he said quietly.

It is difficult to speculate on Ahab's reason for this friendly gesture. It might have been a brief gesture of kindness, or it might have arisen from the wish to prevent any sign of disagreement between himself and the first mate to be evident to the crew. Either way, Ahab's orders were carried out.

Luckily, after much searching, the leaky casks were found. It was extremely fortunate that a typhoon had not yet occurred, because the ship would have had a difficult time withstanding it in the disarray caused by the search.

Chapter 13: Queequeg's Coffin

Very soon after the leaky cask search, poor Queequeg contracted a dangerous fever. It was thought that he would die. He became extremely thin, and it seemed like he would waste away to only his frame and tattoos. While his body grew leaner and sharper, however, his eyes became wider, softer, and more lustrous, as if he had made contact with the divine. One experienced a feeling of awe while looking at him in this state. He rested quietly in his hammock.

One day, he called Ishmael to him, to give certain instructions. When he died, he did not want to be thrown overboard wrapped in his hammock, as was the custom. He hated the thought of the sharks eating him. He mentioned that when he was in Nantucket, he saw that whalemen who died there were laid in dark canoes and peacefully floated away. He wanted a similar end. He asked that the carpenter be requested to make him a dark canoe, with a special lid. He wanted the head section to be able to be opened, so his eyes and face would be exposed to the starry sky.

The order to the carpenter was accordingly given. He came to duly measure Queequeg, he gathered the necessary materials, and then he went to work. When he had completed the coffin, he brought it to Queequeg, so it could be approved or disapproved. When he was on his way to do so, several of the men saw him and tried to drive him away. They could not bear seeing their poor friend and comrade's final resting place, and they thought Queequeg would find it particularly disheartening, as well. Queequeg heard this loud disagreement, and called out that he insisted the coffin be brought to him. He must see it.

The carpenter entered the room and put the coffin on the floor. Queequeg silently and thoughtfully looked at it. He then asked for his harpoon. He took the iron part of it and placed it in the coffin along with one of the paddles of his boat. He then requested that biscuits and a flask of fresh water be placed at the head and that a piece of sail cloth be rolled up for a pillow. After all this was done, he asked to be lifted out of his hammock and into his coffin, so that he might make a trial of its comforts. After he had been moved accordingly, and he was quiet a few moments, he asked that a wooden representation of one of the gods of his religion, Yojo, be given to him. He put Yojo on his chest and crossed his arms around the statue.

A little while passed, and he indicated that the coffin was appropriate and asked to be put back in his hammock. However, before anyone had a chance to carry out this request, Pip, who had been hovering around all this while, holding a beloved tambourine, began to speak.

"Poor rover! Will you never be done with all this weary roving? Where will you go now? But if the currents carry you to those sweet islands with the water-lilies, will you do one little errand for me? Seek out one Pip, who has now been long missing. I think he's there. If you find him, comfort him. He must be sad. For look, he's left his tambourine behind! I found it." Pip begins to play the tambourine. "Queequeg, if you die now, I'll beat you your dying march."

Starbuck and Ishmael heard this awful strange speech. Starbuck commented in a very quiet voice, "I have heard that in violent fevers, people have spoken in ancient languages they have no known familiarity with and that when the mystery is investigated, it turns out that in their forgotten childhood those ancient tongues had truly been spoken in their hearing. And so, poor Pip, in this strange sweetness of lunacy, brings heavenly confirmation of our final homes. He gained this wisdom when he was close to death, in the immense ocean."

Ishmael thought about this quietly and deeply. Starbuck was also speechless. They were, therefore, startled when Pip began to speak again, but in a more animated and agitated way than before.

"Let's make a General of him! Queequeg dies brave! Queequeg dies courageous! But base little Pip, he died a coward, died shivering. If you find Pip on the island with the water-lilies, tell everyone he is a runaway and a coward. Tell them he jumped from a whale boat! I'd never beat my tambourine over base Pip, and hail him General. Shame on all cowards! Let them drown like Pip, that jumped from a whale boat. Shame! Shame!" exclaimed Pip.

Starbuck and Ishmael looked at one another in concerned, saddened amazement. Queequeg was still in his coffin, and his eyes were closed. It seemed as if he were in a dream. Pip was led away, and the sick man was moved to this hammock.

After all this, it is amazing to relate that, to everyone's joy, Queequeg actually rallied and recovered from his illness! What happened to his coffin, you ask? In a mood of wild whimsy, Queequeg made it into a sea chest and kept all his clothes and possessions within it!

Chapter 14: Perth, the Blacksmith

After having to witness such a sad, melancholy scene in the previous chapter, it may seem harsh to read yet another sad story here. This story is the life of Perth, the Blacksmith. The blacksmith might not seem an important figure in this story. He may not have seemed an especially significant figure on the ship itself. But his story of sadness and escape to the sea echo those of countless other sailors.

Perth was an elderly man, and looked even older than he was. He seemed to struggle when he walked. At the age of sixty, he experienced ruin: ruin of his family and his business. He had married later than other men tended to, and had three young children. He and his family were happy. Every Sunday, they went to a cheerful church, situated in a pretty grove.

One night, a burglar entered their house, which also contained his forge. This thief took a fantastic deal. So much, in fact, that from this point poor Perth was never able to get his business back on its feet. It seemed like each catastrophe invited another. In the end, he lost his wife and children to illness. There he was, a man of sixty who had lost everyone he had left in the world. Passing people dismissed him as a nameless vagabond.

Some might say that death seems the only desirable sequel for a tragedy like this. But death is only a launching into the region of the strange unknown and untried. To Perth's death-longing eyes, the always receptive and welcoming ocean allured him as a way of escaping the world while still alive. He buried himself in a life at sea.

Chapter 15: The Ship of Merriment

One day, the Pequod came upon a ship called the Bachelor. It was a Nantucket ship that had done wonderfully well on the whale hunt and would soon be on its way home. It had killed so many whales and obtained so much oil that they struggled to wedge in the last cask of oil.

If the Bachelor had already completed its hunt, and could now go home, why was it not yet sailing in that direction? Why, because the captain and crew wanted to display their success and celebration to other, perhaps less successful captains and crews!

The three men at the Bachelor's mast-head wore long red streamers on their hats, and a brazen, bright lamp was nailed to the ship's main trunk. The sound of enormous drums and fiddle music came from the ship. The crew was joyfully celebrating its success.

The stranger captain called to Ahab. "Come aboard!" he exclaimed, cheerfully. He lifted a glass and bottle in the air!

Ahab felt extremely irritated and asked his usual question. "Have you seen the White Whale?" He gritted the question through his teeth.

"No. I've only heard of him, but I don't believe in him at all! Come aboard!" said the stranger captain, good-humoredly.

"You are too jolly," Ahab said grumpily. "Sail on. Have you lost any men?"

"Not enough to speak of," was the stranger captain's strange and careless answer. "But come aboard, old hearty. Come along! I'll soon remove that darkness from your brow. Come along!"

"How wondrously and ridiculously familiar is the fool," muttered Ahab to himself. He then spoke more loudly. "You are a full ship and homeward bound, you say. Well, then, call me an empty ship and outward-bound. So go your way, and I will mine. Forward!"

Consequently, while the Bachelor went cheerfully before the breeze, the Pequod stubbornly fought against it. The Pequod's crew looked at the departing Bachelor and its joyous crew in a grave, lingering way.

Perhaps good luck can sometimes be contagious! The day after encountering the jolly ship, the Pequod caught four whales! To Ahab's disappointment, however, not one of them was Moby-Dick.

Chapter 16: Fedallah's Prophecy

Very late the night of the day they caught four whales, everyone on the Pequod was asleep except for those on watch and the mysterious Fedallah. He was watching the sharks swimming around one of the dead whales they had caught that day.

Down in his cabin, Ahab was woken from sleep by a terrible nightmare. It was a dream he had had before. He knew he could sleep no more that night, and decided to make his way to the deck, to breathe the night air and ensure the men on watch were being vigilant.

When he reached the deck, he came face to face with the Fedallah. Surrounded by the gloom of the night, they seemed the last men in the world.

"I have dreamed it again," said Ahab, suddenly and without any other greeting.

"Of the hearses? Old man, have I not said that neither hearse nor coffin can be yours?" asked Fedallah.

"But who are hearsed that die at sea?" answered Ahab.

"Neither hearse nor coffin can be yours," Fedallah repeated. "But I said, old man, that before you could die on this voyage, two hearses must be seen by you on the sea. The first, not made by mortal hands, and the last must have visible wood grown in America," stated Fedallah.

"Aye, aye! A strange sight that, Parsee. A hearse and its plumes floating over the ocean with the waves for the pall-bearers. Ha! This is a sight we will not see soon," laughed Ahab. "And what did you say regarding yourself?" he asked.

"I shall die before you, and after my death I must appear to you. This must happen before you may die," stated Fedallah, coolly.

"Ah! This all sounds very likely," joked Ahab.

Fedallah looked at Ahab directly. His eyes lighted up like fire-flies in the gloom. "Only rope can kill thee," he said.

Ahab laughed again. "The gallows, you mean? I am immortal then, on land and on sea!"

Both men were now silent, as silent as one man alone.

Chapter 17: Starbuck's Struggle

A terrible typhoon arose! The Pequod, while tossed violently on the water, made it through without any injuries to the crew. However, the ship sails needed repair. They also needed adjustment, in order to keep Captain Ahab's ordered course. The repairs to maintain the course were done by Starbuck. He felt gloomy and frightened because he knew the closer they got to the White Whale and the realization of Ahab's hunt, the closer they were to danger and probable death!

On the Pequod, any time any kind of change was made on deck, the mates were required to notify Captain Ahab. So, Starbuck went down to the captain's cabin.

The captain's cabin had both an outer and inner room. Starbuck could access the outer room without knocking, but the inner room, where Ahab usually sat and slept, was bolted. He paused before knocking at this inner door. He was not sure why he did so.

The inner room's door had a window at its top. It was covered only with thin blinds, and Starbuck could easily see through the wide spaces they left clear. He could see that Captain Ahab was sleeping.

The outer room's ceiling lamp was swinging back and forth, with the force of the waves. It casted strange shadows on the bolted door. The outer room also held the musket rack. As we know, Starbuck was generally a fair and honest man. Yet when he saw the muskets, an evil thought entered his mind. He began to murmur to himself.

"He would have shot me once," he said quietly yet angrily to himself. "There's the musket he aimed at me." He touched that musket and lifted it off the rack. He began to shake. "He would have killed me with this musket. Yes, and if he's allowed, he will kill all the crew. He is crazy. He is leading us to our death, all for vengeance on the cursed White Whale. We will all die for vengeance on a dumb animal, if he has his way. Yes, if this ship comes to deadly harm, it will make him the murderer of more than thirty men."

Starbuck then heard Ahab mumbling in his sleep. The mate began to talk quietly to himself again.

"In there he sleeps. He is sleeping, yes, but still alive. He will wake up soon. He will continue to demand absolute obedience. He will not listen to reason!   A touch on this musket and I may survive to hug my wife and child again. But if I do not wake you to death, old man, we will all soon sink to the bottom of the ocean!"

Starbuck is shocked out of his dangerous state by Ahab shouting loudly in his sleep. "Oh Moby-Dick, at last I clutch your heart!", he yelled.

Starbuck's shaking arm placed the musket back on the rack, and he left the cabin. He returned to the deck and spoke to Stubb.

"Mr. Stubb, the captain is in a deep sleep. Would you go down there and wake him up? You know what to do and say to wake him up. I must stay here."

Chapter 18: A Strange Use for a Coffin!

You may be thinking that Queequeg has already made a strange use of his coffin! After all, the last you heard was that he was keeping his clothes in it! Yet, it came to pass that an even stranger use was made of what was supposed to be his final resting place.

On Ahab's orders, the Pequod was heading towards the Equator. The ship was drawing near to the outer areas of the Equatorial fishing ground. One early morning, a member of the crew who had been assigned to the watch out for the White Whale climbed up the mast head while still groggy from sleep. Sadly, the poor man fell off the mast and into the ocean. The life-buoy, a wooden flotation device attached to the ship with a spring, was tossed to him. Unfortunately, with the darkness of his surroundings and the panic of his heart, he was not able to get hold of it and he drowned quickly. He never surfaced at all.

This sad event occupied the minds of everyone on board. Also, they realized that the life-buoy which had been thrown to the poor sailor was now shriveled by the strong sunlight that had been long beating upon it by the time it was located.

The life-buoy needed to be replaced as quickly as possible. Starbuck was assigned this task, but he could not find a wooden cask light enough to serve the purpose. Then something odd happened. Queequeg began to make strange hints concerning his coffin! Starbuck was horrified.

"A coffin, for a life-buoy!" Starbuck cried, staring at Queequeg in disbelief.

"A very strange idea," said Stubb.

Flask then joined the conversation. "It would serve the purpose."

Everyone except Queequeg stared at him as if he had gone mad.

Flask did not flinch. "The carpenter could easily arrange it," he continued, calmly. Everyone was silent for a few moments. Finally, Starbuck spoke.

"Very well. Bring it up," he said.

The others now stared strangely at him!

"There's nothing else to be done!" he explained.

Queequeg brought up his coffin, and the carpenter was summoned. He was told to nail down the lid, and seal the seams. When the assignment was fully explained to him, the carpenter was rather offended! He viewed this work as that of a tinker rather than a carpenter. After all, a carpenter makes objects out of raw materials, while it is the humble tinker who makes something out something else — a coffin, for example! However, the work was done, and the coffin used as an unusually dreary life-buoy!

Chapter 19: Captain Gardiner

The next day, the Pequod met a large ship called the Rachel. A pleasant man named Captain Gardiner was it commander.

As the Rachel moved closer and closer to the Pequod, the first thing the Pequod's men noticed was that its masts were covered in men, like tree branches covered with cherries! They could not believe how many men had been assigned to the Rachel's look-out. In fact, they were quite befuddled by the sight.

When the Rachel was close enough, its captain got into a boat and came to greet Captain Ahab. As the boat drew nearer, Captain Gardiner became aware that he recognized Ahab as a fellow Nantucketer! His sad situation made him relieved to see a familiar face.

Captain Gardiner was about to shout a greeting when Ahab abruptly asked, "Have you seen the White Whale?" Captain Gardiner was a bit taken aback by the abruptness and strangeness of this question, but answered politely.

"Yes, I have. Yesterday, in fact." He then took a moment to catch his breath, and asked Ahab his own question.

"Have you seen a whale-boat adrift?"

Ahab struggled to conceal his joy at the information he had just received, and calmly replied that no, he had not seen such a thing. He wanted to be rid of the stranger captain, and be on his way, but poor Captain Gardiner motioned that he wanted to come aboard and the three mates and the men helped him do so. This friendly captain greeted Ahab again. Ahab did not acknowledge him or the fact that he did indeed recognize the stranger captain.

"Where did you see him? Was he not killed? Not killed?" cried Ahab, with a crazed expression in his eye.

Captain Gardiner was alarmed by Ahab's frantic tone of voice and facial expression. It took him a moment to collect himself.

"We saw and pursued him yesterday afternoon," answered Captain Gardiner. One of our boats actually succeeded in harpooning and fastening him." Gardiner's already somber and apprehensive facial expression became as frightened and pale as a lost ghost. "The whale sped off, dragging the boat after him until it disappeared from sight. We could not catch up with them, and we could not find them the whole day and night, no matter how hard we looked. We have lowered boats several times, and, as you can see, we have many look-outs. They simply cannot be found." His eyes now filled with tears. This was unusually emotional behavior for a sea captain. It drew the close attention of the Pequod's mates. Captain Gardiner swallowed, took a few deep breaths, and then continued. "My son, my own boy is in that boat. He is just twelve years old! Please, I beg you, please let the Pequod join me in the search! With another ship on the search, we can cover a much larger area. Please. You must help me! If necessary, I will pay you for use of the ship." He looked at Ahab with pleading, desperate eyes. Ahab, however, was icy. He did not seem to care at all.

Stubb immediately spoke. "His son! What do you say, Ahab? We must save the boy, of course!" Ahab was silent.

"I will not leave until you say yes. Imagine yourself in my situation. I know that you have a boy, Captain Ahab. A child of your old age. I would help you, no matter what the cost!" cried Gardiner.

"Captain Gardiner, I will not do it. Even now, I lose time. Good bye, and God bless you, man. May I forgive myself. I must go," was Ahab's cruel and astonishing answer.

Gardiner was stunned. As if he was starting from a spell, he silently hurried to the side of the ship. He fell rather than stepped into his boat, and then returned to his ship.

The Pequod's three mates and the other members of the crew who had witnessed it were appalled at Ahab's cruelty. It was evident that his relentless quest for the White Whale had destroyed his humanity and compassion. Starbuck was terrified.

The sad Rachel went on its halting and winding way.

Chapter 20: Sympathy

Three days passed after meeting the Rachel, and the White Whale had still not been seen. Ahab began to imagine that his crew had actually seen the whale and were not telling him, in order to avoid the hunt! He was especially anxious about Starbuck's influence. So, he decided to mount the masts himself, along with the rest of the men on look-out! For a captain to do this was almost unheard of!

The first time that Ahab did this, a large black sea hawk quickly appeared and, for some reason, took a liking to the captain's black floppy hat! It grabbed the hat and flew off with it, followed only by Ahab's loud insults! When the bird had reached a far distance, it must have changed its mind as it dropped the hat into the middle of the ocean! The men who saw this could not help but think this was a sign of bad things to come for their captain. Starbuck was among them.

One clear, blue day, Starbuck saw Ahab leaning over the side. The captain leaned as if he had a heavy weight on his back. One solitary tear fell from his face and into the ocean. He wore a black, slouchy hat exactly like the one he had lost! He looked terribly old. Starbuck felt sorry for him and approached him quietly. After a few moments, Ahab realized that he was standing beside him.

"Starbuck!" he exclaimed.

"Sir," answered the mate.

"Oh, Starbuck! It is such a wonderful, beautiful day! The wind and sky are so mild, and the air seems enchanted. It was a day just like this, forty years ago, that I caught my first whale. I was eighteen years old. Forty years ago! Starbuck, do you know that of those forty years I have not spent as many as three ashore? I have lived a life of desolation and solitude. And now look at me. I chase my prey like a demon! Why do I do this? But it is unfair that, with this load I bear, one of my poor legs was stolen from me! Do I look old? Will you please brush aside this grey hair from my eyes? It seems to make them water and weep." Starbuck did as he was asked.

"These grey hairs mock me. I have not lived enough to have them." He paused for a few moments. "Starbuck, let me look into your eyes. Looking into a human eye is better than anything else in this world. Starbuck, when my boat is lowered to kill Moby-Dick, you must stay onboard ship. Do not share my danger!" Ahab said.

Starbuck stared at the captain with amazement and gratitude. "My captain! You have a noble heart! But why should anyone chase that monstrous whale? Let me alter the ship's course! Let us go home!" he exclaimed.

Starbuck had felt a glimmer of hope. In the end, however, he could not convince the captain. Ahab turned his head away from the mate, and was silent. He then said simply, "It is fate. It cannot be changed."

Starbuck's face turned deathly pale. Despair overtook him. He left. When Ahab turned around later, he discovered that the mate was gone. The captain then aimlessly walked to the other side of the deck and gazed into the water. He was met with an unnerving image of the eyes of Fedallah. The man was leaning over the same rail. The image was his eyes' reflection.

Chapter 21: The White Whale

The further the ship moved on its course, the more certain Ahab was that Moby-Dick would be spotted at any moment. Even at night, he insisted there be at least one man on look-out duty, and every morning his immediate question to the numerous men on the masts was if they had seen the White Whale.

By this point in the voyage, Ahab insisted on being hoisted up to the mast-head every day. He would not put complete trust in the eyesight and honesty of his crew. Besides, he thought, he was the man destined to find and conquer Moby-Dick, and so he was most fit and likely to spot him!

One morning, immediately upon reaching this height, he suddenly stared and gasped. He then cried out, "There he blows! There he blows! The color of a snow-hill! It's Moby-Dick!" He and the other men on the masts could see the White Whale was about a mile in the distance.

"Did any of you see him before?" Ahab asked.

Tashtego spoke up, and said "I saw him almost that same moment as you did, sir. Did you not hear me cry out?"

"Not the same moment. No, the doubloon is mine. Fate decreed I shall have it, as fate decreed I shall kill the White Whale." He paused less than a moment. "Prepare three boats! Mr. Starbuck, remember that you are to stay on the ship. All boats ready?"

Ahab, Stubb, and Flask then entered their boats with their crews and were lowered down onto the water. As they quietly paddled, it seemed like the White Whale had not noticed their presence. He glided serenely through the mild tropical sea. After a period of time, Ahab came so close to the whale, he could clearly see the animal's dazzlingly white humped back, as well as the milky shadow from his wrinkled, broad forehead. White sea birds often like to congregate above and around where a whale is in the water, and this was the case today.

After a while, the whale began to show more of himself by raising the front part of his body slowly from the water. Soon, his whole body formed a high arch. He looked as if he were made of marble! When he thus revealed himself, he sounded and then went out of sight. It seemed like a warning to all but Ahab.

"An hour," said Ahab, indicating how long he thought it would be before the whale reappeared. In a moment, the water began to swell.

"The birds! The birds!" cried Tashtego. The white birds were flying towards Ahab's boat! Ahab looked down into the sea but could not see anything. However, as he peered down more intensely, he perceived something about the size of a white weasel. As he continued to look, the white creature became bigger and bigger and bigger and turned into a giant! It was Moby-Dick! Moby-Dick with an open jaw, heading with speed upwards to the bottom of Ahab's boat!

Ahab used his steering oar in an attempt to move the boat out of the whale's terrifying path. He picked up his harpoon. The whale, however, with what seemed a supernatural intelligence, moved to the side in an instant, placing himself immediately under Ahab's boat once again. In an instant, Ahab's boat was cradled in the whale's mouth! Soon, the craft broke in half. All the crew fell into the water. All but Ahab managed to grab hold of a part of the boat.

The fact that Ahab had only one real leg made it difficult for him to swim, but he was just able to keep his head above water. Moby-Dick now began to circle the boat and crew, each time getting closer and closer.

The two other boats were unharmed, but they were afraid to attack the whale in case that angered it into immediately killing Ahab and the others. Luckily, however, the Pequod was travelling quickly to the scene. When it was close enough, Ahab yelled "Sail against the whale! Drive him off!" The ship tried to do exactly that, and succeeded. The whale was gone.

Chapter 22: Fedallah's Fate

The next day, the men on the mast-heads cried out that they saw a jet from Moby Dick's spout. They said that the whale was a far distance from the ship. After a few minutes had gone by and there was no other sign of the whale's presence, however, Ahab insisted on mounting the mast as well, insisting that Moby-Dick does not cast one jet and then completely disappear!

Ahab was right! The reality was that the men had been mistaken in what they thought they had seen. They were wrong because Moby-Dick was not in the distance. In fact, he was much nearer to the ship than they could have ever imagined! His body burst into view! He had risen with incredible speed and power straight from the bottom of the ocean to its surface! When a whale did this, it was called "breaching". It was unusual and rather aggressive. The giant whale then tossed himself like a salmon in the air!

The three boats were lowered, and Starbuck again told to stay on the ship. Ahab instructed him to keep the ship closer to the boats than was usually the custom.

As soon as the boats were in the water, Moby-Dick, with open jaw, turned and sped towards them! It seemed a declaration of war. In an instant, the whale was furiously swimming and thrashing among the boats! Harpoons were being darted at him from every boat, but he was able to ignore them! He seemed determined to destroy each and every boat. The whale tangled all the lines from the various harpoons together, by swimming in different directions. He was then able to dash about the boats against each other. Ahab realized that he must cut his part of the line, and did so.

During all this time, the captain and men could barely see a thing. The whale's thrashing created a great deal of white water, foam, and mist as you can imagine. Flask and Stubb's boats were completely emptied, the men floundering in the water. Moby-Dick then positioned his forehead under Ahab's boat and crashed against it! The boat was sent into the air, where it turned over and over. It fell into the water upside down, and Ahab and his crew had to struggle out from under it.

The ship approached more closely in order to try to carry out a rescue, and the whale sped off. Ahab, Flask, Stubb, and all the men were taken onto the ship. When they reached the deck, everyone was staring at Ahab. He was leaning on Starbuck's shoulder, as his ivory leg had been snapped off! Again, the White Whale had taken unfortunate Ahab's leg!

Starbuck and other men encouraged Ahab to sit down and rest, which he did. Suddenly, Ahab's eyes grew wide.

"Gather the men. Surely I have not seen him yet? It cannot be! Find Fedallah!" Ahab cried.

They went away and searched thoroughly. They could find no sign of him. Stubb spoke quietly.

"Sir, I thought I saw him get caught in the tangles of the lines. I thought I saw him dragged under by the whale," said Stubb.

Starbuck could no longer remain silent.

"Captain Ahab, all of this is madness. The whale has taken your leg again. He has destroyed boats. He has killed Fedallah! These are warnings. Please, for your own sake and for all of us, give this up!" begged Starbuck.

Ahab turned away. Then he spoke.

"This hunt was rehearsed by you and me a billion years before this ocean came to be. Fate cannot be changed!" Ahab replied, with a mad look in his eyes.

Again, Starbuck walked away.

The carpenter made Ahab a new leg out of wood from the captain's broken boat.

Chapter 23: The Pequod's Fate

On the third day of this wild pursuit of Moby-Dick, Ahab realized early in the morning that the ship was now going in the opposite direction of the whale's current path. He ordered the ship to be turned, and it, therefore, had to sail against the wind rather than in harmony with it.

"He struggles against the wind to find the open jaw," muttered Starbuck to himself. "My bones already feel damp" he continued, grimly.

When the whale was finally spotted, Captain Ahab ordered three boats be lowered. Again, Starbuck was to stay on the ship. When Ahab was about to get into his boat, he looked at Starbuck and spoke.

"I am old. Shake hands with me, man," Ahab said.

Starbuck gave his hand.

"My captain, do not go" begged Starbuck.

Ahab ignored this plea.

"Lower away!" the captain cried.

Maddened by the new iron that corroded in him, Moby-Dick was formidable. He thrashed among the boats, causing as much destruction as he could! As the whale moved about, a sudden cry rang out among all the men. Ahab dropped his harpoon. There, in front of them, was the torn body of Fedallah! He was tied to the whale's back by the tangled rope. His dead eyes looked up into Ahab's. It all suddenly dawned on the captain. The whale was the hearse made by no man.

Soon, Ahab darted his harpoon at the whale. The angry and distressed animal flew forward. Somehow, in the convoluted movements of the whale and Ahab's foolish attempts at maintaining his hold on the whale, the rope wrapped around Captain Ahab's neck. He was pulled into the sea so quickly that his crew hardly saw it. They sat in shock. The captain was with the whale and Fedallah in the ocean! The captain was dead.

Noise from the ship broke their trance. The whale, evidently seeing the ship as the source of all his pain and persecution, had attacked it. If Ahab had been alive to see this, he would have known that the ship, made of American wood, was the second hearse!

Tashtego could be seen at the top head-mast of the ship. He stood there, unmovable. He looked as if he did not know that the ship was sinking, that many of his crewmates had already drowned, and that soon the place where he stood where be at the bottom of the ocean.

Soon, the ship sank. Everyone we have met in this story was in the ocean, but one. This one person was Ishmael. As if something divine was watching over him, the coffin life-buoy appeared, floating beside him. He held onto this object for two days, until he was finally rescued. The ship who rescued him? The lost Rachel. Still searching for the missing child, she found an orphan.

Made in the USA
Middletown, DE
16 June 2023

32733404R00066